PAPERCUTZ

Graphic Novels Available from
PAPERCUTZ

Graphic Novel #1
"Prilla's Talent"

Graphic Novel #2
"Tinker Bell and the Wings of Rani"

Graphic Novel #3
"Tinker Bell and the Day of the Dragon"

Graphic Novel #4
"Tinker Bell to the Rescue"

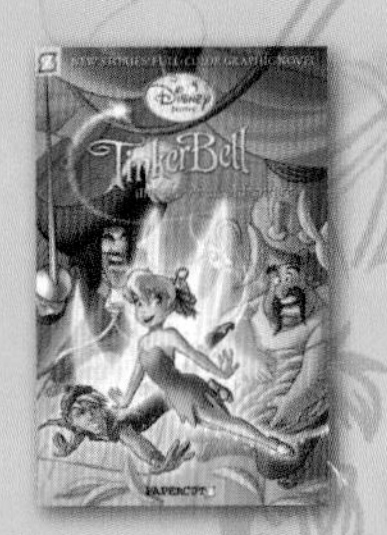

Graphic Novel #5
"Tinker Bell and the Pirate Adventure"

Graphic Novel #6
"A Present for Tinker Bell"

Graphic Novel #7
"Tinker Bell the Perfect Fairy"

Graphic Novel #8
"Tinker Bell and her Stories for a Rainy Day"

Graphic Novel #9
"Tinker Bell and her Magical Arrival"

Tinker Bell and the Great Fairy Rescue

Coming Soon:

Graphic Novel #10
"Tinker Bell and the Lucky Rainbow"

DISNEY FAIRIES graphic novels are available in paperback for $7.99 each; in hardcover for $12.99 each except #5, $6.99PB, $10.99HC. #6-10 are $7.99PB $11.99HC. Tinker Bell and the Great Fairy rescue is $9.99 in hardcover only. Available at booksellers everywhere.

See more at www.papercutz.com

Or you can order from us: please add $4.00 for postage and handling for first book, and add $1.00 for each additional book. Please make check payable to NBM Publishing. Send to: Papercutz, 160 Broadway, Suite 700, East Wing, New York, NY 10038 or call 800 886 1223 (9-6 EST M-F) MC-Visa-Amex accepted.

#9 "Tinker Bell and Her Magical Arrival"

Contents

The Magical Arrival 5

A New Talent 20

The Magic in You 35

A Fairy Might Be Near 50

PAPERCUTZ™
NEW YORK

"Magical Arrival"
Script: Augusto Macchetto
Revised Dialogue: Cortney Faye Powell
Pencils: Antonello Dalena
Inks: Manuela Razzi
Color: Kawaii Creative Studio
Letters: Janice Chiang
Page 5 art:
Pencils and Inks: Stefano Attardi
Color: Caterina Giogetti

"A New Talent"
Script: Augusto Macchetto
Revised Dialogue: Cortney Faye Powell
Pencils: Antonello Dalena
Inks: Manuela Razzi
Color: Kawaii Creative Studio
Letters: Janice Chiang
Page 20 Art:
Pencils and Inks: Sara Storino
Color: Stefano Attardi and Andrea Cagol

"The Magic in You"
Script: Augusto Macchetto
Revised Dialogue: Cortney Faye Powell
Pencils: Antonello Dalena
Inks: Manuela Razzi
Color: Kawaii Creative Studio
Letters: Janice Chiang
Page 35 Art:
Pencils and Inks: Sara Storino
Color: Stefano Attardi and Andrea Cagol

"A Fairy Might Be Near"
Script: Augusto Macchetto
Revised Dialogue: Cortney Faye Powell
Pencils: Antonello Dalena
Inks: Manuela Razzi
Color: Kawaii Creative Studio
Letters: Janice Chiang
Page 50 Art:
Pencils and Inks: Manuela Razzi
Color: Andrea Cagol

Nelson Design Group, LLC – Production
Special Thanks – Shiho Tilley
Michael Petranek – Associate Editor
Jim Salicrup
Editor-in-Chief

ISBN: 978-1-59707-323-3 paperback edition

ISBN: 978-1-59707-324-0 hardcover edition

Printed in China
August 2012 by Asia One Printing LTD
13/F Asia One Tower
8 Fung Yip St., Chaiwan
Hong Kong

Distributed by Macmillan

First Papercutz Printing

COME ON, TINK! TELL IT AGAIN!
AGAIN?! AREN'T YOU TIRED OF HEARING THE STORY OF MY ARRIVAL?
NO WAY! IT GETS BETTER EVERY TIME YOU TELL IT!
WELL, IF YOU INSIST...

THE MAGICAL ARRIVAL
IT IS A COLD AND GRAY WINTER ON THE MAINLAND, BUT SPRING IS JUST AROUND THE CORNER.
AND SOON THERE WILL BE FLOWERS, AND LIGHT, AND BRIGHT COLORS... THANKS TO FAIRIES!

IT ALL BEGINS WITH A BABY'S FIRST LAUGH. FOR THAT IS HOW A FAIRY IS BORN!

HA HA HA HA HA HA!

THE LAUGHTER TAKES OFF...
HAHAHAHAHA
...CARRIED BY A DANDELION WISP...

HAHAHAHAHAHAHAHAHAHA

...THROUGH THE NIGHT SKY...
HAHAHAHAHAHAHA

...ALL THE WAY TO THE ISLAND OF *NEVER LAND*...
HAHAHAHAHAHA

...AND FINALLY, TO PIXIE HOLLOW, WHERE THE FAIRIES LIVE!
HAHAHAHAHAHAHAHAHAHAHAHA
HAHAHAHAHA

THE FAIRIES GATHER TOGETHER TO GREET THE LAUGHTER...
HA HA HA
HA

THEN, ALL IT TAKES IS A LITTLE PIXIE DUST...
HA
HA
HA
HA
HA

...AND THE LAUGHTER CARRIED BY THE DANDELION WISP IS MAGICALLY TRANSFORMED INTO A FAIRY!

FOR SUCH A SPECIAL OCCASION, **QUEEN CLARION** HERSELF WELCOMES THE NEW FAIRY!
WELCOME TO PIXIE HOLLOW!
AND NOW YOU HAVE TO FIND YOUR TALENT!
THE ICON THAT SHINES THE BRIGHTEST WILL REVEAL THE FAIRY'S TALENT...
OH! W-WHAT ARE THESE?
EVERY FAIRY HAS A **TALENT...** SOMETHING THAT SHE IS **ESPECIALLY WELL-SUITED** FOR! THESE OBJECTS WILL HELP YOU RECOGNIZE YOURS!

WHEN THE NEW FAIRY GENTLY TOUCHES THE FLOWER...
HUH?
POOF
...THE FLOWER SUDDENLY WILTS AND DIMS. *CLEARLY* FLOWERS ARE NOT HER TALENT.

AND NEITHER IS WATER!
POOF

IT'S NOT EVEN SPEED!

BUT FINALLY...
WOW! LOOK HOW IT SHINES!
YOU'RE A *TINKER* FAIRY!

HOW ABOUT GIVING *TINKER BELL* A WARM WELCOME? SHE'S ONE OF YOURS!
HI! I'M *BOBBLE* AND HE'S *CLANK.* FLY WITH US. WE'VE GOT LOTS TO SHOW YOU!

THE TINKERS ESCORT THE NEW FAIRY AS THEY FLY THROUGH THE FREEZING WINTER WOODS...
IT'S ALMOST TIME FOR THE CHANGING OF THE SEASONS!
YOU'RE RIGHT! THE WINTER FAIRIES ARE RETURNING TO NEVER LAND FOR REST!
WHEN THEY REACH A GRASSY VALLEY, TINKER BELL SEES FAIRIES ARE PAINTING LADYBUGS TO PREPARE THEM FOR SPRING...
THE OTHER FAIRIES ARE USING THEIR TALENTS TO BRING SPRING TO THE MAINLAND.
AND FINALLY, THEY REACH TINKER'S NOOK...
!
THIS IS WHERE WE LIVE AND WORK... AND FROM NOW ON, IT'S YOUR HOME, TOO!

THERE'S *YOUR HOUSE!*
OH! WOW!

COME ON IN! WE'VE GOT SOME CLOTHES FOR YOU...
THOUGH THEY MAY BE A LITTLE BIG!
COME JOIN US WHEN YOU'RE READY! *FAIRY MARY* WILL WANT TO MEET YOU!

A LITTLE BIG? I'D SAY IT'S HUGE!

HMM...

A FEW WING BEATS LATER...
LOOKING GOOD!
YEAH, BUT WHO IS IT?

IT'S TINKER BELL, SNAIL-BRAIN!
OOOHHH!

YOU'RE ALL PRETTY BUSY, AREN'T YOU?
OF COURSE! WE'RE TINKERS AND WE FIX AND INVENT THINGS!

WE CARVE ACORN BUCKETS...
...AND WE MAKE BUSHELS...

AND BASKETS, TOO... OUCH!
BEING A TINKER IS NEVER A BORE!
KLONK

WE HELP ALL THE OTHER FAIRIES WITH OUR INVENTIONS!
BUT WE'VE GOT TO DELIVER THEM! HAVE YOU REPAIRED THE WAGON?
UM... YES, FAIRY MARY!

NOW YOU HAVE TO MEET TINKER BELL!
WHO?

SHE'S NEW, FAIRY MARY...
I LOOK FORWARD TO FLYING WITH YOU!

WONDERFUL, A NEW FAIRY! LET ME SEE YOUR HANDS!
?

SUCH DELICATE HANDS! BUT DON'T WORRY...

SOON YOU'LL HAVE MUSCLES LIKE A REAL TINKER FAIRY. OKAY, LET'S GET BACK TO WORK!
SURE!

HELPING WITH THE DELIVERY, TINKER BELL SOON MEETS THE OTHER FAIRIES...
WE'VE BROUGHT YOU YOUR RAINBOW TUBES, IRIDESSA!
FANTASTIC! CAN YOU GIVE ME A HAND, SILVERMIST?
SURE!

TINKER BELL EAGERLY WITNESSES AN AMAZING PROCESS: FIRST SILVERMIST, A WATER FAIRY, THROWS A FINE MIST OF WATER INTO THE AIR. THEN IRIDESSA, A LIGHT FAIRY, FLIES THROUGH THE WATER CREATING A NEW RAINBOW WITH HER PIXIE DUST...
WOW! WHAT ARE YOU GOING TO DO WITH THAT RAINBOW?

TAKE IT TO THE MAINLAND!
?

UHM... WHAT'S THE MAINLAND?
IT'S THE PLACE WE HAVE TO DELIVER SPRING TO, DEAR.

I'LL PAINT THE FLOWERS THERE!
WAY TO GO, ROSETTA!

AND I'LL BRING FOOD FOR MY ANIMAL FRIENDS!
OF COURSE, FAWN! YOU SEE TINK...

...WE JUST FOLLOW THE SECOND STAR...
...AND FLY OVER THE OCEAN...
...ALL THE WAY TO THE MAINLAND!
TINKER BELL IS EXCITED AND AMAZED BY HER NEW FRIENDS, AND IMAGINES IT WOULD BE AN INCREDIBLE JOURNEY TO GO TO THE MAINLAND...

BUT NOT ALL THE FAIRIES ARE SO FRIENDLY...
UHM...HI! YOU MUST BE VIDIA RIGHT? MY NAME'S TINKER BELL...
HA! THE NEW ONE...

WHAT'S YOUR TALENT?
WHAT DO YOU THINK?
WOOOSH

UH... ARE YOU A POLLEN GATHERER?
I'M A FAST FLYING FAIRY! IT'S A VERY RARE TALENT, YOU KNOW!

I MAKE THE WIND BLOW! INCLUDING THE WIND THAT BROUGHT YOU HERE!

WELL, EVEN WE TINKER FAIRIES ARE PRETTY USEFUL...
OH, IS THAT SO?

!
I UNLEASH THE FORCES OF NATURE... WHILE YOU *FIX* POTS!

DON'T TAKE IT SO HARD, SWEETIE! THE ARRIVAL OF *SPRING* CERTAINLY DOESN'T DEPEND ON YOU...
OH, YES IT DOES!

WHEN I GO TO THE MAINLAND, I'LL PROVE TO EVERYONE HOW *IMPORTANT* TINKER FAIRIES ARE!
AND THAT IS THE STORY OF HOW TINKER BELL CAME TO PIXIE HOLLOW. BUT AS WE ALL KNOW, TINKER BELL HAS A LOVE FOR ADVENTURE THAT WILL NOT BE DENIED. SEE FOR YOURSELF IN THE NEXT STORY...!

THE END

IT'S HARD TO BELIEVE YOU EVER WANTED TO BE ANYTHING OTHER THAN A TINKER-TALENT FAIRY...
I *KNOW!* I WAS YOUNG AND SILLY-- BUT YOU KNOW THE STORY...

A NEW TALENT
TINKER BELL, THE NEWEST FAIRY, HAS JUST ARRIVED IN PIXIE HOLLOW, WHERE THE FAIRIES LIVE! BOBBLE AND CLANK, HER NEW TINKER FRIENDS, ARE TEACHING HER ALL ABOUT HER NEW LIFE AS A TINKER-TALENT FAIRY...
IT'S TIME TO GET READY FOR QUEEN CLARION'S REVIEW!
WHAT'S THAT, BOBBLE?
IT'S A VERY EXCITING TIME OF THE YEAR IN PIXIE HOLLOW! FAIRIES ARE WORKING VERY HARD TO BRING THE SEASON OF SPRING TO THE MAINLAND!
QUEEN CLARION WILL BE CHECKING ON WHAT THE FAIRIES HAVE PREPARED FOR SPRING!
AND TINKER FAIRIES WILL PROVE THEY'RE WORTHY OF SUCH AN HONOR!

TINKER BELL IS SO EXCITED! SHE CAN'T WAIT TO GET TO THE MAINLAND AND NOW SHE'LL BE ABLE TO SHOW HOW IMPORTANT TINKERS ARE...
HERE'S MY BIG CHANCE...

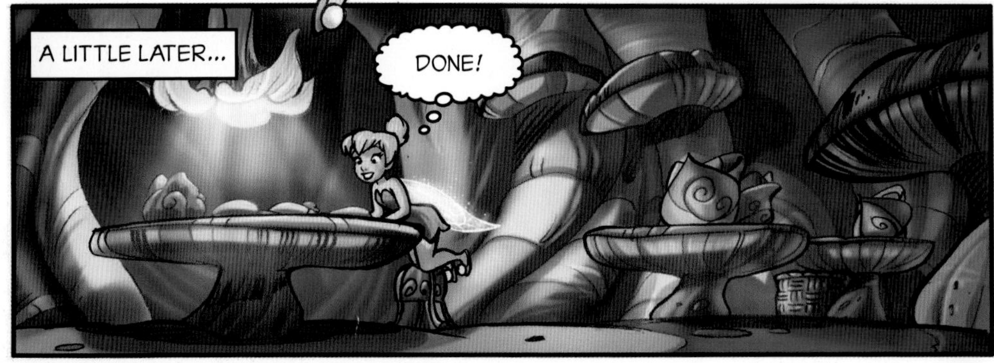
A LITTLE LATER...
DONE!

SOON, EVERYTHING'S READY IN *SPRINGTIME SQUARE* FOR THE QUEEN'S REVIEW...

THE MINISTER OF SPRING, THE MEMBER OF THE FAIRY COUNCIL RESPONSIBLE FOR ENSURING THAT SPRING COMES AND GOES IN AN ORDERLY MANNER, FINALLY ANNOUNCES...
THE QUEEN IS COMING! STRIKE UP THE BAND!

QUEEN CLARION, YOUR EXCELLENCY! WELCOME TO SPRINGTIME SQUARE!

BUT WHILE THE MINISTER OF SPRING LEADS QUEEN CLARION TO INSPECT ALL THE PREPARATIONS TO BRING SPRING TO THE MAINLAND...
EVERYTHING'S ALL SET, YOUR MAJESTY! AS SOON AS THE **EVERBLOSSOM** BLOOMS, WE'LL SET OUT TO...
?
RUMBLE
WHAT...
QUEEN CLARION! HAVE I MISSED ANYTHING?

I CAME UP WITH SOME THINGS THAT TINKER FAIRIES CAN USE ON THE *MAINLAND!*
SWISH
AN UNEASY MURMUR RIPPLES THROUGH THE CROWD, BUT TINKER BELL IS TOO EXCITED TO NOTICE...
TINKER FAIRIES ON THE MAINLAND?!
OH, NO! NO ONE'S TOLD HER THAT--
TO BEGIN WITH, THIS WILL HELP YOUNG SQUIRRELS OPEN THE ACORNS! *UHM...*
CLACK
ERR... I STILL HAVE TO PERFECT IT!
SPROING
BUMP
SQUEEK!

THIS IS A FLOWER PAINTER! LOOK, MINISTER...

OOPS! SORRY!
SPLOOSH
SPROING

TINKER BELL, DEAR... DIDN'T ANYONE TELL YOU?
TELL ME WHAT?

THAT TINKER FAIRIES DO NOT GO TO THE MAINLAND! THEIR WORK IS HERE IN PIXIE HOLLOW!

BUT I THOUGHT...
I'M SORRY!

OH, OKAY... NO, THAT'S... GOOD! I MEAN I REALLY COULDN'T MAKE IT ANYWAY, SO... GOOD. YEAH. SO, I'M JUST GONNA...UM... GO NOW.
A DEVASTATED FAIRY RETURNS TO TINKER'S NOOK...
WHY CAN'T WE GO TO THE MAINLAND, FAIRY MARY?
TINKER BELL, ARE YOU A GARDEN FAIRY? OR A LIGHT FAIRY?
NO!
OF COURSE YOU'RE NOT! ONLY WHEN YOU MAKE FLOWERS BLOOM, OR CAPTURE A SUNBEAM, WILL YOU BE ALLOWED TO GO TO THE MAINLAND!
SUDDENLY, TINK SMILES AGAIN...
HMM...
UNTIL THAT DAY, YOUR PLACE IS HERE!

THE NEXT DAY, TERENCE, THE DUST-KEEPER FAIRY, PASSES OUT PIXIE DUST, AS HE DOES EVERY DAY. THE FAIRIES NEED IT TO FLY...
HERE YOU GO, SILVERMIST!
THANKS, TERENCE! HEY, I HOPE TINK'S OKAY!

POOR THING! SHE LOOKED SO DOWN-HEARTED YESTERDAY!
MORNIN' GIRLS!

TINKER BELL!
I'VE MADE UP MY MIND. I'M NO LONGER GOING TO BE A TINKER FAIRY!

MAYBE I CAN CHANGE MY TALENT!
CHANGE TALENTS? GEE... I DON'T KNOW, TINKER BELL!
IF YOU WOULD TEACH ME YOUR TALENT, ROSETTA, THE QUEEN WOULD LET ME GO TO THE MAINLAND!
WELL, YOU COULD TRY!
BUT I'VE NEVER HEARD OF A FAIRY CHANGING HER TALENT BEFORE, FAWN!
IRIDESSA'S RIGHT!
IT'S JUST THAT... YOU WORK SUCH WONDERFUL MAGIC! AND I... WANT MORE OUT OF LIFE THAN MAKING POTS AND PANS!

OKAY! I'LL HELP YOU!
OH, THANKS, SILVERMIST!

ME, TOO!
WELL, THERE'S A FIRST TIME FOR EVERYTHING.

SO TINKER BELL'S TRAINING AS A WATER FAIRY BEGINS...
WELL, THEN... FOR YOUR FIRST DAY AS A WATER FAIRY, YOU'LL LEARN HOW TO MAKE WAVES... OR...

HEY! I GOT IT!

I'LL TEACH YOU HOW TO PUT DEWDROPS ON SPIDER WEBS!
OHHH! YES!
GOOD LUCK, TINKER BELL!

JUST CUP YOUR HANDS AND...

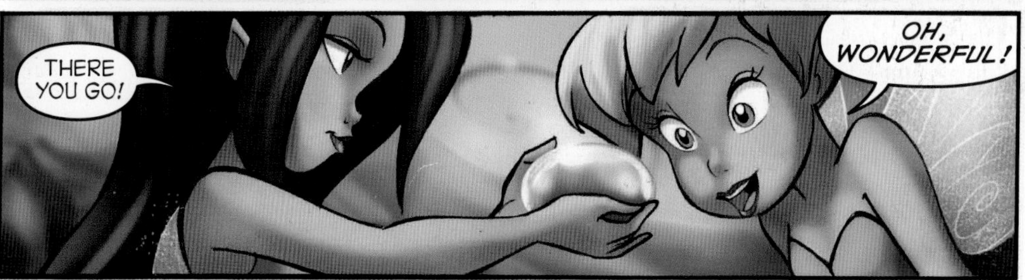
THERE YOU GO!
OH, WONDERFUL!

NOW COMES THE TRICKY PART...

PUTTING THE DEWDROP ON THE SPIDER WEB! THERE!
PLIP

NOW... WHAT HAPPENED TO YOUR DROP?
FORGOT IT... HEE HEE!

OKAY...

HEY, I DID IT... AHH!
POP

DON'T WORRY ABOUT IT! YOU CAN DO IT!
YES!
HUH...?
POP
OH, NO!
ALL THE DEW DROPS POP! EXCEPT FOR THE LAST ONE...
THERE!
SPROING

WHICH BOUNCES BACKWARD!
ARGH!
SPLASH

YOU KNOW, TINKER BELL, YOU MIGHT CONSIDER BECOMING A *LIGHT FAIRY!*
HUH?!

WILL TINKER BELL SUCCEED IN FINDING A NEW TALENT?
THERE ARE DEFINITELY LOTS OF OTHER TALENTS TO TRY OUT IN PIXIE HOLLOW! AND THE MORE YOU DISCOVER, THE MORE ENTICING THEY GET!
THE END

NOT EVERYONE CAN BE GREAT AT **EVERYTHING!** I SURE FOUND OUT THE HARD WAY!
THAT'S TRUE! BUT YOU ALSO FOUND OUT SOMETHING MORE IMPORTANT!

THE MAGIC IN YOU
THE NEWEST FAIRY IN PIXIE HOLLOW, IS A TINKER FAIRY NAMED TINKER BELL...
EVERY FAIRY HAS A TALENT. SOMETHING SHE'S ESPECIALLY GOOD AT DOING. BUT TINKER BELL IS UNHAPPY WITH HER OWN TALENT.
WHAT CAN I TEACH YOU, TINK?
SHE RECENTLY DISCOVERED THAT TINKER FAIRIES ARE NOT ALLOWED TO GO TO THE MAINLAND, WHICH IS SOMETHING SHE DESPERATELY WANTS. SO, SHE HAS DECIDED TO SWITCH TALENTS WITH THE HELP OF HER FAIRY FRIENDS...

I'VE GOT IT! WE'LL GATHER UP THE LAST LIGHT OF DAY! HERE, TAKE THIS BUCKET!

GOOD! NOW, GO TO IT! GATHER THE LIGHT!

HERE'S MINE!
WOW!

BUT, I DIDN'T GET ANY!
NO PROBLEM!

NOW COMES THE FUN PART! FOLLOW ME!

BABY FIREFLIES LOVE LIGHT! IT'S LIGHT FAIRIES WHO GIVE THEM THEIR GLOW...
COME ON, TAKE IT EASY!

ZAP
ZAP
IT'S ALL YOURS!

ARE YOU READY, GUYS?

OH, NO! I CAN'T GET THE LIGHT!

MAYBE YOU SHOULD GIVE UP...?
NO! I'LL GET IT!

WATCH OUT!
UMPF!

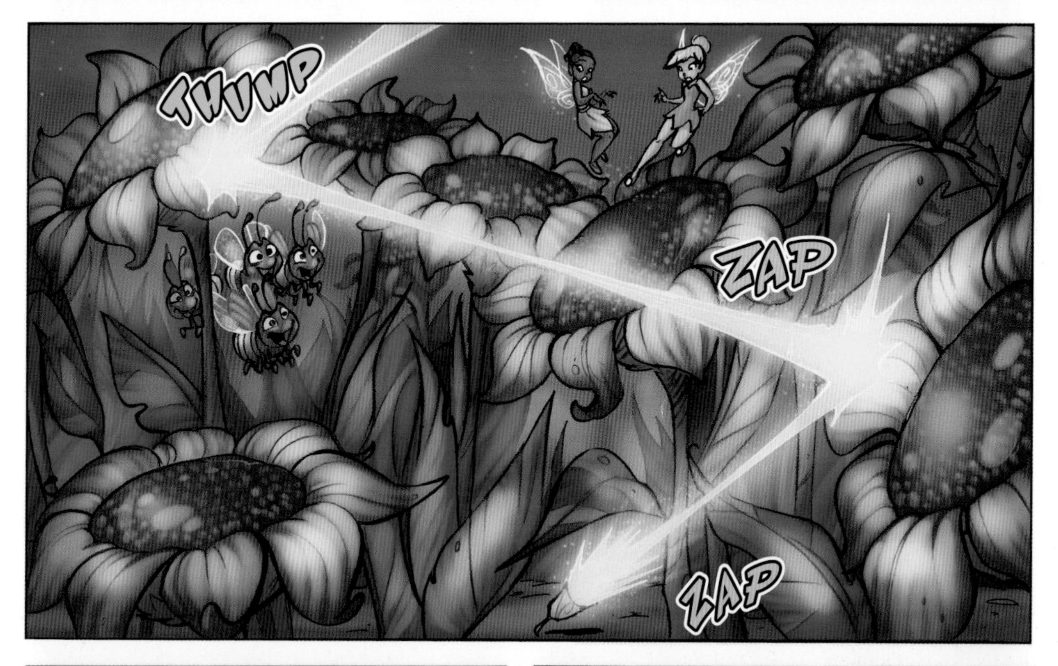
THUMP
ZAP
ZAP

HEY!

FLY, TINKER BELL! FLY!

TINKER BELL RETURNS TO HER FELLOW TINKER FAIRIES...
WELL, LOOK WHO'S HERE! WELCOME BACK!
UM... I'VE BEEN BUSY, FAIRY MARY!

I KNOW VERY WELL WHAT YOU'VE BEEN UP TO! CHANGING TALENTS... I'M DISAPPOINTED WITH YOU!

HOW COULD YOU, TINKER BELL?!
SO WHAT? I DON'T WANT TO SPEND THE REST OF MY LIFE FIXING THINGS!

OH! I DIDN'T MEAN TO OFFEND EITHER OF YOU... I...

...HAVE TO BE GOING!

THE NEXT MORNING, FAWN, AN ANIMAL-TALENT FAIRY, TEACHES TINKER BELL HER TALENT...
WE'LL TEACH THE BABY BIRDS HOW TO FLY! REMEMBER, YOU HAVE TO SMILE...

...AND ESTABLISH TRUST!

WHY DON'T YOU TRY WITH THAT LITTLE ONE?
OH, RIGHT! UM...

OKAY, SMILE... AND ESTABLISH TRUST...
!

HI, THERE! YOU WANNA DO SOME FLAP-FLAP TODAY?

BUT THE BABY BIRD DOESN'T EVEN WANT TO HEAR ABOUT IT!
OUCH!
GNAP

HE IS SO FRIGHTENED...
COME ON, LITTLE GUY! DON'T YOU WANT TO FLY WITH ME?

...HE JUST WANTS TO GO BACK INSIDE HIS EGG!
HM... THIS CALLS FOR AN IDEA!

OH, LOOK AT THAT BIG BIRD FLYING UP HIGH! HE'LL HELP US!
!

I'LL CALL HIM! CAW! CAW!

SCREECH!

OH, NO! THAT'S A HAWK TINKER BELL! FLY FOR IT!

SCREECH!

WHAT LUCK... A HIDING PLACE!

THIS IS MY HIDING SPOT!
VIDIA!

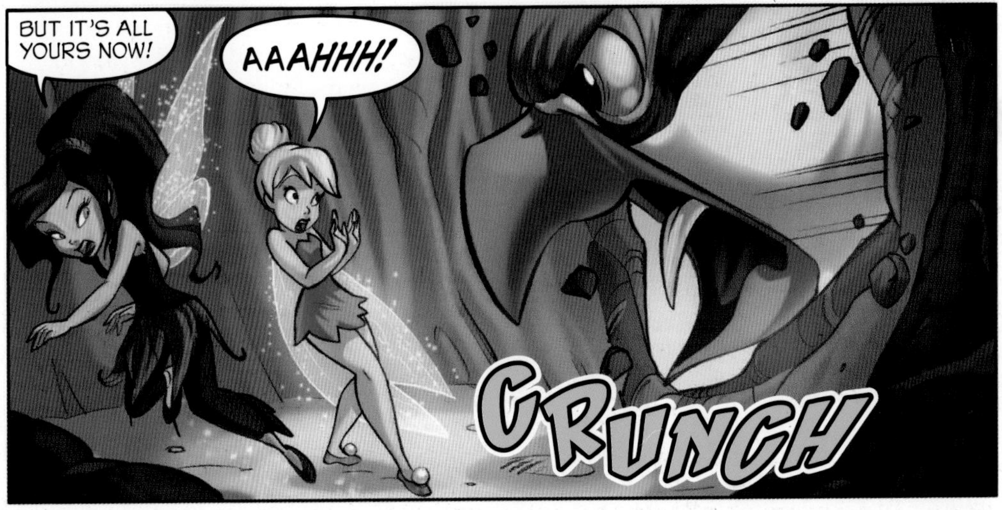
BUT IT'S ALL YOURS NOW!
AAAHHH!
CRUNCH

GOOD THING THERE'S STRENGTH IN NUMBERS...
FLY AWAY!

BOP
BOP
BOPPITY
BOP

IN NO TIME, THE FAIRIES MANAGE TO GET RID OF THE HAWK!

BUT TINKER BELL IS DISAPPOINTED...
SIGH I CAN'T DO LIGHT TRICKS! BABY BIRDS HATE ME...

WE HAVE TO HELP HER!
OH, I'M USELESS!

LATER...
LOOKS LIKE I'LL ALWAYS BE A TINKER FAIRY!

AND I'LL NEVER GO TO THE MAINLAND!

?
CLINK

OH! WHAT DO WE HAVE HERE?

TINKER BELL HAS STUMBLED UPON SOME LOST THINGS FROM THE MAINLAND THAT HAVE WASHED UP ON THE SHORE OF NEVER LAND...
WHAT COULD THEY BE?

QUICKLY, TINKER BELL'S TALENT TAKES OVER... GATHERING ALL THE PARTS LYING AROUND IN THE DIRT, SHE FIXES THE MYSTERIOUS GADGET IN A WING BEAT! SOMETHING NO ANIMAL TALENT OR LIGHT TALENT FAIRY COULD DREAM OF DOING!
CLING
CLACK

UH?

HEY, WHAT'S THAT?
SHHH!

HERE YOU GO!

AND NOW...

I'VE FIXED IT! *SUCCESS!*
IT'S BEAUTIFUL, TINKER BELL!
LIKE MAGIC, THE DANCER STARTS TO SPIN AS MUSIC BEGINS TO PLAY...

HEY! WHAT ARE YOU DOING HERE?
IT'S SPLENDID, BUT WHAT IS IT?

I DON'T KNOW. I JUST *FIXED* IT!
OF COURSE YOU DID!

YOU'RE A *TINKER FAIRY*-- YOU HAVE A TALENT FOR FIXING THINGS!

ISN'T THAT WHAT YOU LIKE DOING, TINKERING?
SURE! WHO CARES ABOUT GOING TO THE MAINLAND?

I DO! I WANT TO GO THERE! ROSETTA, AREN'T YOU GOING TO TEACH ME TO BE A GARDEN FAIRY ANY MORE?

OH, TINKER BELL, I THINK ***TINKERING*** IS YOUR SPECIAL TALENT!

YES, AND WE DO WANT YOU TO BE ***HAPPY!***
THEN HELP ME CHANGE MY TALENT! YOU PROMISED!

TINKER BELL MAY LIKE TO FIX THINGS... BUT SHE STILL HAS HER HEART SET ON THE MAINLAND...
PLEASE, TINKER BELL, THINK ABOUT WHAT WE'VE SAID! ALL RIGHT?
MAYBE TINKER BELL WILL GET TO GO ONE DAY. THERE ARE STILL MORE TALENTS TO TRY...
THE END

SOMETIMES WHEN YOU WANT SOMETHING **SO MUCH,** YOU DON'T GET IT!
BUT, WHEN YOU ACCEPT THAT YOU MAY NOT GET IT-- SUDDENLY, LIKE MAGIC, YOU DO GET IT! JUST LIKE IN THIS STORY...

TINKER BELL HAS JUST ARRIVED IN PIXIE HOLLOW, THE PLACE IN NEVER LAND WHERE FAIRIES LIVE. BUT TINKER FAIRIES, LIKE TINKER BELL, DO NOT GET TO GO TO THE MAINLAND, SO TINK DECIDED SHE'LL CHANGE HER TALENT!

BUT MAYBE SHE SHOULDN'T LISTEN TO VIDIA... SHE'S A SPITEFUL FAIRY!
WELL, IF YOU REALLY WANT TO BE A GARDEN FAIRY...

"'CAPTURE THE SPRINTING THISTLES...' OKAY. I CAN DO IT!"
READY, CHEESE? THERE'S ONLY 7 OR 8 AT THE MOST!
A FAIRY MIGHT BE NEAR

A SMALL GROUP OF SPRINTING THISTLES IS SLOWING ITS RUN...
OKAY! GOT 'EM...

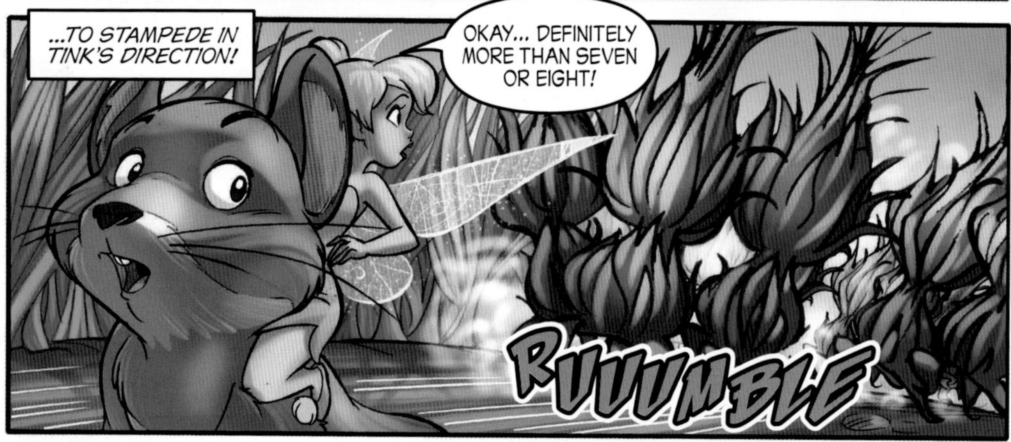
...TO STAMPEDE IN TINK'S DIRECTION!
OKAY... DEFINITELY MORE THAN SEVEN OR EIGHT!
RUUUMBLE

GOOD THISTLES, INTO THE CORRAL YOU... OOOH!
CRASH

UNFORTUNATELY, A LITTLE WHILE LATER...
OH, NO! THE THINGS WE'VE PREPARED FOR SPRING!
SAVE THE SEEDS!
CRASH
SORRY. SORRY. 'SCUSE ME! SO SORRY!
IT'S TINKER BELL!

TINKER BELL! WHAT WERE YOU TRYING TO DO?
I WANTED TO TAME THE SPRINTING THISTLES AND...

THIS TIME YOU'VE REALLY GONE OVERBOARD, TINKER BELL!
BUT NO GARDEN-TALENT FAIRY KNOWS HOW!

BY THE SECOND STAR! WHO'S RESPONSIBLE FOR THIS MESS?
I AM, QUEEN CLARION! SORRY... IT'S ALL MY FAULT!

WITH THE PREPARATIONS RUINED, THE FAIRIES WON'T BE ABLE TO BRING SPRING TO THE MAINLAND...
EVERYTHING OKAY, TINKER BELL?
YES, BUT I NEED A QUICK REFILL. I'M GOING AWAY FOR A WHILE!
OH? FOR HOW LONG?
WELL, ACTUALLY... FOREVER!
FOREVER'S A LONG TIME! YOU'RE GOING TO NEED A LOT OF PIXIE DUST!

THANKS, TERENCE?
YOU REMEMBER MY NAME?

WHY SHOULDN'T I?
WELL, I'M JUST A DUST-KEEPER!

NOT THE MOST IMPORTANT FAIRY IN PIXIE HOLLOW.
ARE YOU KIDDING? YOU'RE THE MOST IMPORTANT ONE THERE IS!

WITHOUT YOU, NO ONE WOULD HAVE ANY MAGIC!

YOUR TALENT MAKES TOU WHO YOU ARE! YOU SHOULD BE PROUD OF IT!
I AM!

WHAT TINKER BELL SO CLEARLY SEES IN TERENCE, SHE'S UNABLE TO SEE IN HERSELF...

LATER, IN HER WORKSHOP...
PROUD... PROUD OF WHAT?
I COULDN'T EVEN GET THESE SILLY THINGS TO WORK...
UNLESS... SURE! WHY NOT?!

TINKER BELL RUMMAGES THROUGH THE PILE OF TRINKETS SHE HAS FOUND ON THE BEACH AND THEN...
LOST THINGS! THAT'S IT!

MEANWHILE, IN SPRINGTIME SQUARE...
ATTENTION, EVERYONE, I'M AFRAID I HAVE **BAD NEWS.** THERE IS NO WAY SPRING CAN COME ON TIME.

"MONTHS OF WORK WERE LOST. I'M AFRAID WE WON'T BE GOING TO THE MAINLAND THIS YEAR!"
WAIT!

TINKER BELL, THIS IS NEITHER THE TIME OR THE--
I KNOW HOW WE CAN FIX *EVERYTHING!*

PLEASE, HEAR ME OUT! YOU!
?

HOW LONG DOES IT TAKE YOU TO PAINT A LADYBUG?
UM... TEN, FIFTEEN MINUTES!

OH, YEAH? WELL, *LOOK* AT THIS!
PFFFT

WHOA! THAT WAS FAST!

SEE? WE CAN PAINT, GATHER SEEDS, AND DO EVERYTHING ELSE MUCH QUICKER!

BUT I CAN'T DO IT ALL BY MYSELF!

I'LL HELP!
I'LL HELP!
COMMAND US, TINKER BELL!
THANKS, EVERYBODY! LET'S GET TO WORK! GATHER TWIGS OF ALL SIZES, TREE SAP AND, MOST IMPORTANTLY... LOST THINGS!

THANKS TO TINKER BELL'S TALENT, SOON EVERYTHING IS READY FOR THE MAINLAND!
YOU DID IT, TINKER BELL! YOU'VE SAVED SPRING!

QUEEN CLARION, CAN TINK COME WITH US TO THE MAINLAND?
NO, NO! MY WORK IS HERE! AND I STILL HAVE SO MUCH TO DO...
NOT HERE, YOU DON'T!

?
YOU FIXED THIS, REMEMBER?

I RAN ACROSS THIS MYSELF MANY SEASONS AGO BUT I DIDN'T HAVE A CLUE AS TO HOW TO FIX IT.
YOU ARE QUITE A RARE TALENT INDEED!

SOMEONE LOST THIS AND HERE IS A TINKER FAIRY WITH A JOB TO DO ON THE MAINLAND! BRING THIS THING HOME!
ME?!

HOW WILL I FIND WHO IT BELONGS TO?
YOU'LL KNOW! NOW GO!

AT LAST, TINKER BELL AND THE FAIRIES SET OFF FOR THE MAINLAND, BRINGING SPRING WITH THEM!

THEY WORK THEIR MAGIC ON FLOWERS...
...AND FIELDS...
WAKE UP, SLEEPYHEAD!

AT SUNSET...
OH! IT'S GLOWING! WE MUST BE CLOSE BY!

HERE WE ARE!
TAP
TAP

WHAT'S THIS? OH! ***MUMMY! MUMMY!***

YES, ***WENDY,*** WHAT IS IT, DARLING?

*PERCHANCE YOU FIND A TOY YOU LOST, OR JINGLING BELLS YOU HEAR... IT ALL MEANS THAT ONE **VERY SPECIAL FAIRY** MIGHT BE NEAR!*
THE END